To Alysia

Easter 1989

March 26

From Mommy & Daddy

Adam Raccoon
at
Forever Falls

Glen Keane

Chariot Books
DAVID C. COOK PUBLISHING CO.

In memory of
Marcey Brandt

ALYSIA
Marie
HOLOWELL

Chariot Books is an imprint of David C. Cook
Publishing Co.
David C. Cook Publishing Co., Elgin, Illinois 60120
David C. Cook Publishing Co., Weston, Ontario

ADAM RACCOON AT FOREVER FALLS
© 1987 by Glen Keane for text and illustrations

First printing, 1987
Printed in Singapore
92 91 90 89 88 87   5 4 3 2 1

Library of Congress Cataloging-in-Publication Data

Keane, Glen, 1954-
    Adam Raccoon at forever falls

    (Parables for kids)
    Summary: Adam Raccoon and King Aren reenact this
Bible theme, illustrating God's forgiveness of sin and His
wish for our salvation.
    [1. Animals—Fiction. 2. Parables] I. Title. II. Series.
PZ7.K2173Ad   1987   [E]   86-24318
ISBN 1-55513-087-9

Hidden in a faraway corner
of the world lay Master's Wood.

Watching over all who lived in Master's Wood was a mighty lion named King Aren.

And the one he
had to watch the
closest was Adam Raccoon.

Adam, being a playful raccoon,
loved things that sparkled and shined.

"It fits!" Adam shouted.

But when Adam tried to take the crown off, it was stuck tight.

"Do you want some help?"
the king asked Adam.

"No. I can do it myself!" Adam grunted.

Finally, after a lot of
tugging and pushing, Adam
said in a voice you could
hardly hear . . .

"I think I need some help."

King Aren reached down.
POP! The crown came off.

"I think I had better wear this crown," the king said.

swimming!

He floated on his back . . .

and played with his friends.

Adam could swim wherever
he wanted—except . . .

in Tempting Pond, where the
water sparkled and shined.
It was the most beautiful
swimming hole in all of
Master's Wood.

But it was also . . .
the most dangerous!

A swimmer could easily
be swept away
to Forever Falls.

So King Aren put up a sign
that said,
NO SWIMMING

Adam was upset. He wanted
to swim in Tempting Pond.

he dived in!

It was more wonderful than
he imagined.

Aaah! The blue jay was
right.
It did feel good.

Suddenly Adam noticed he
was moving faster. He was
no longer in the pond!

He tried to swim back, but
the current was too strong.

It pulled him farther and farther from the pond, but closer and closer to . . .

Forever Falls.

"Help!" Adam cried as the roar of the waterfall got louder.

Adam's friends heard his cry
and came running.

The bear said, "I can't help
him. I'm too fat. I'd sink."

The rabbit said, "I can't help him. I don't know how to swim."

"And I can't help. I'm too small," said the turtle.

"Who was that?" they all asked.

"KING AREN!"

Forever Falls thundered as
Adam was swept over the edge.
With one last stroke, King
Aren grabbed Adam into his
mighty arms.

He threw Adam back onto shore.

The brave king went over
Forever Falls into the black,
murky water below.

He was gone!

Adam could do nothing but think of how King Aren had given his life for him.

Suddenly . . .

the bushes started
to rustle, and . . .

out came King Aren.
He was alive!

Adam leaped into his arms. "Oh, King Aren. What a fool I was! How can I ever repay you?"

With a smile the king said,
"All that I ask, Adam, is that
you follow me."

And he did.

Do you find yourself telling your children stories to help them understand things you want them to learn or remember? Maybe you find yourself remembering the point of a sermon because of the illustration used.

Telling stories to convey truth is not new. Jesus often taught in parables.

Why do we use parables to teach? Because we *remember* stories—and the truths they hold.

Adam Raccoon and King Aren illustrate truths from God's Word in language and experiences children readily understand. While stories like these are not a substitute for the Bible, they will enhance and reinforce the Bible teaching your children receive.

Adam Raccoon at Forever Falls is a parable about salvation. We see God's love for man illustrated in King Aren's sacrifice for Adam. When you read it with your children, use it to begin a discussion. For example: Of whom does Adam remind you? How is King Aren like Jesus?

How they answer these questions will give you insight into their understanding and open the door to more discussion about God's plan of salvation.

For some children, this story will be one more step in their knowing who Jesus is and their need for salvation. Others may be ready to receive Jesus as their Savior.